Zoom, Rocket, Zoom!

Margaret Mayo & Alex Ayliffe

ORCHARD

Mighty rockets

are good at zoom, **zoom**, **zooming,**

5 4 **3** 2 **1** and . . .

LIFT OFF! Launching!

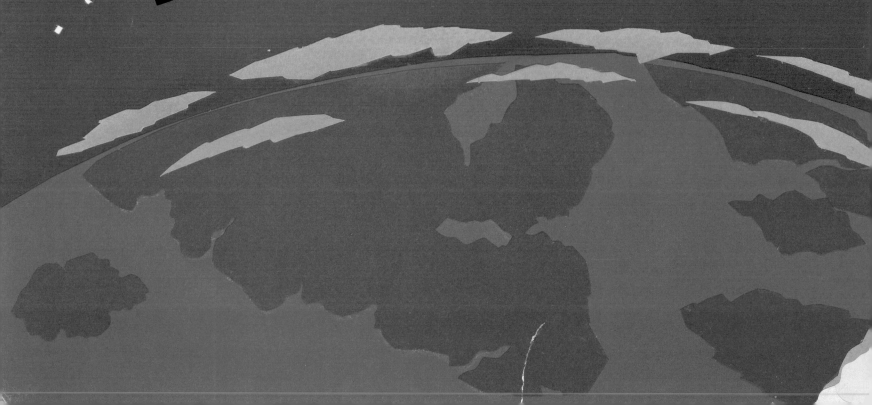

Whoo–oom!

Up they go, zooming.
Blasting into space.

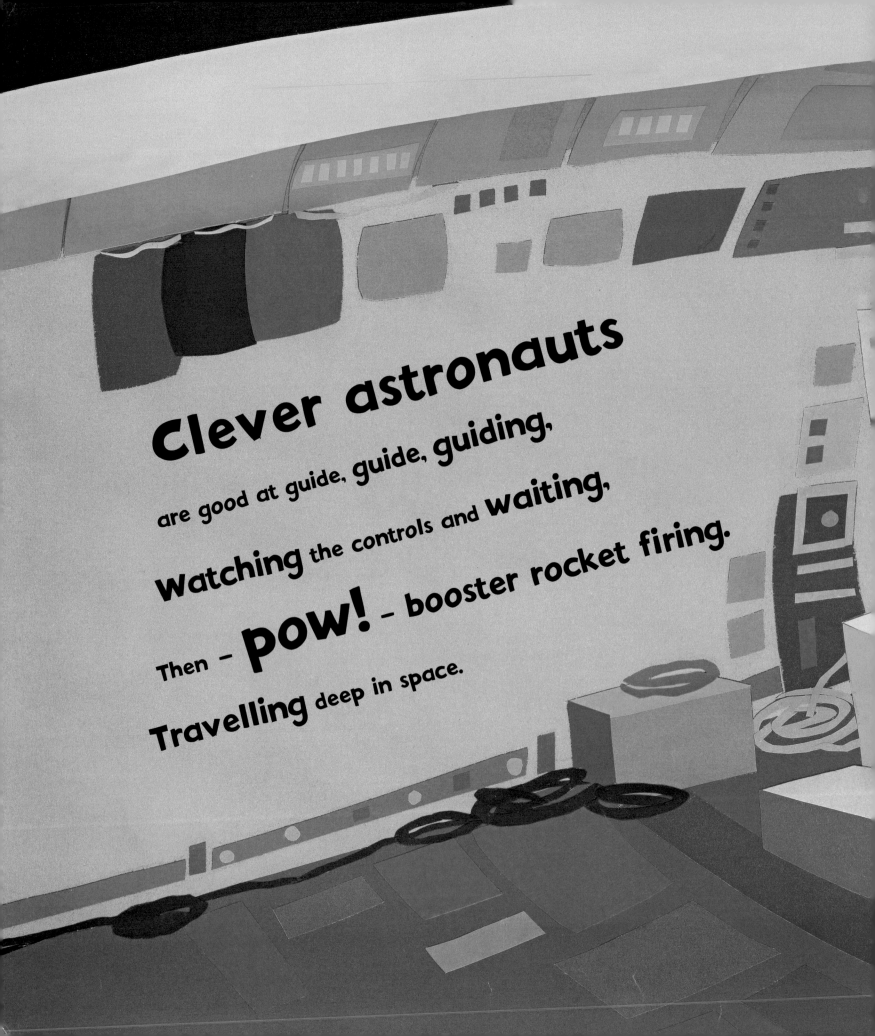

Clever astronauts

are good at guide, guide, guiding,

Watching the controls and **waiting,**

Then – **pow!** – booster rocket firing.

Travelling deep in space.

Lunar modules

are good at **tricky** moon **landings.**

They leave the spaceship, swooping, descending,

Spidery legs ready for – **Bam!** – safe landing.
Touching down in space.

Excited astronauts
are good at moon walking.

Bouncing, bounding . . . Oops! No falling,

As they **SCOOP** up moon rocks, carefully **collecting.**

They can **work** in space.

Moon buggies are good at roll, roll, rolling,
Round wheels turning, soft dust gripping,
Across the humpy, lumpy moon . . . bumpety-bumping.
Driving up in space.

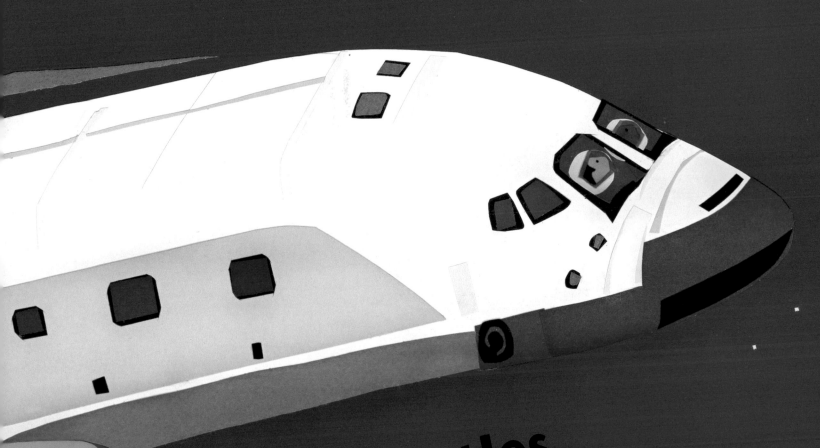

Space shuttles

are good at **big** loads **moving.**

They hurtle upwards, **booming, thundering,**

Off to a **space station** for fast unloading.

Carrying tools through space.

Space stations

are good places for **living**,

Somewhere for eating, **working** and **sleeping**,

And – **whoopee!** – weightless **somersaulting**.

A **home** while up in space.

Bold astronauts are good at space walking.
They have **fun . . .**
arms waving . . . slowly moving . . . almost dancing,

And they can work,
building and repairing.
Floating up in space.

Space satellites

are good at **round-the-earth orbiting,**

Taking pictures for **weather forecasting,**

Signals receiving and – whizz! – to TVs beaming.
Circling up in space.

Robot spacecraft

are good at speed, **speed, speeding,**

Powered by the **sun,** they keep on **flying,**

Reaching distant **planets** and even **landing.**

Moving fast through space.

Robot rovers

are **good** at roam, **roam, roaming.**

They **trundle** over Mars, **searching, measuring,**

Red deserts **finding** and mountains **discovering.**

Exploring deep in space.

When the **night** has **come** and the **moon** shines **bright**,

Reflecting down to **earth** our **sun's** great **light** –

Become a **space explorer!** Watch the **stars** in the **sky!**

And look out for **satellites** . . . just **slowly gliding by!**

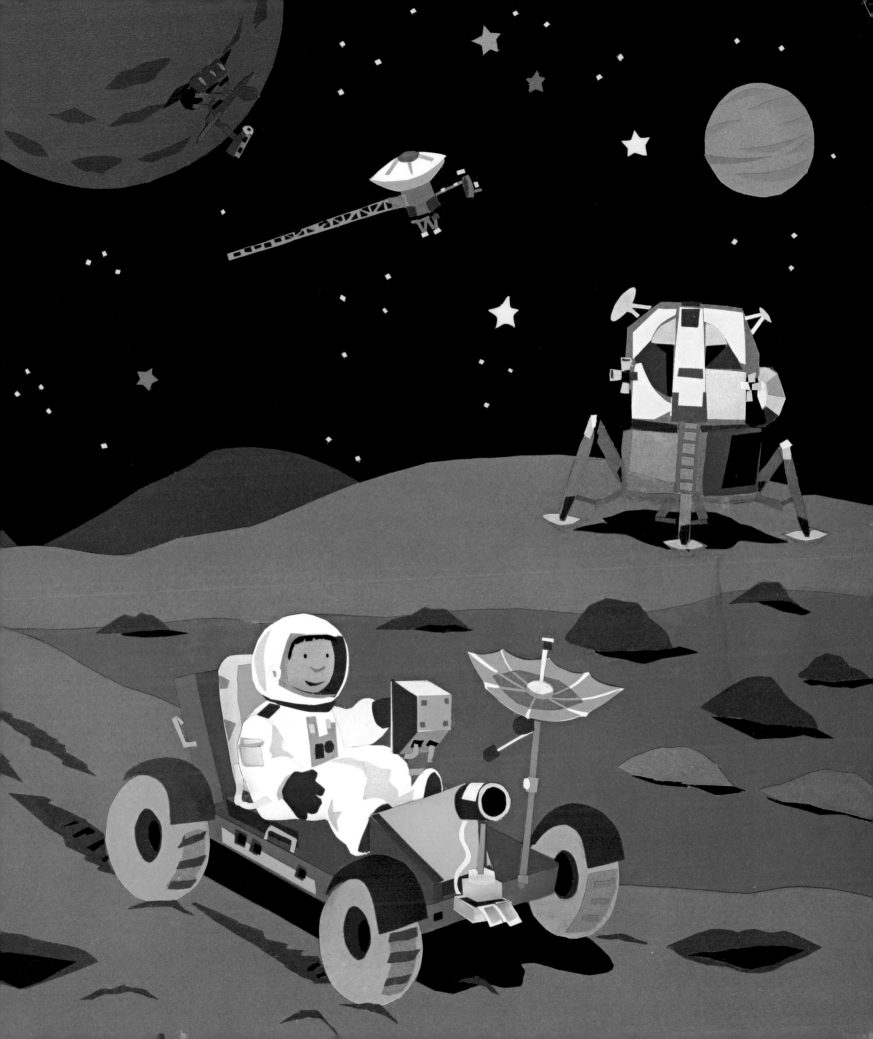

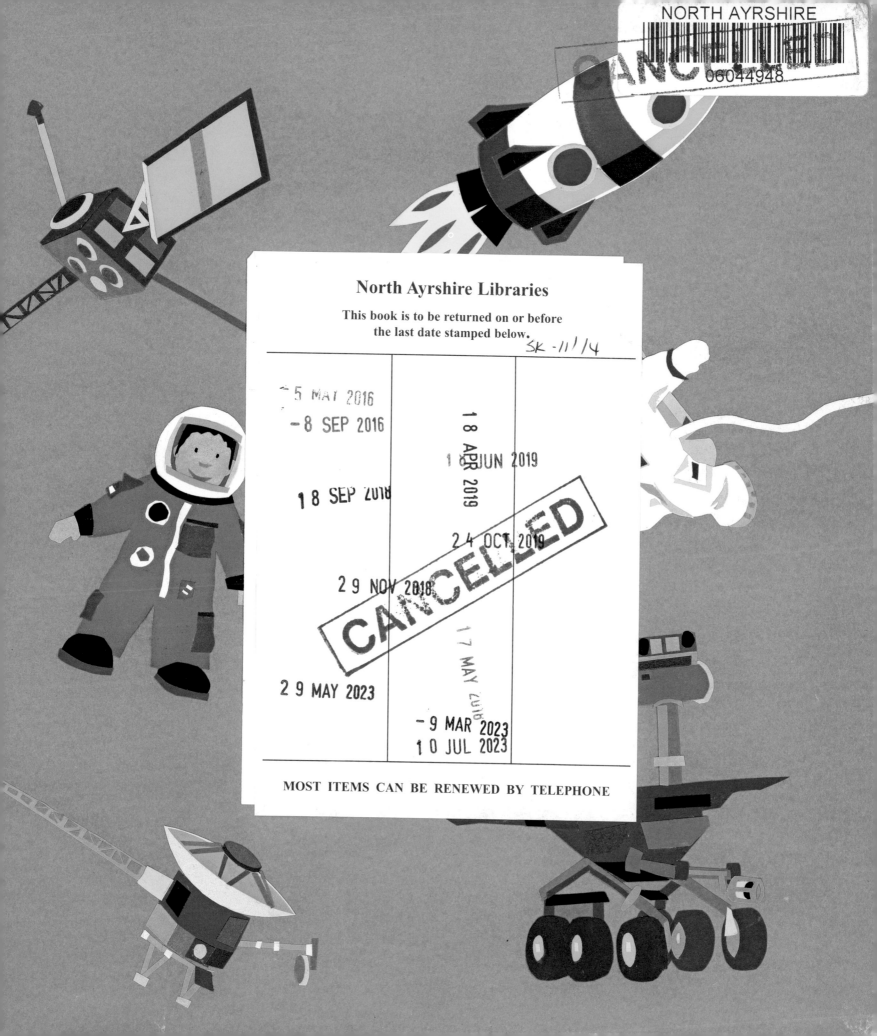

For Beth, Iain, Norman and Sheila
MM

For Tom and Harrison
AA

ORCHARD BOOKS

338 Euston Road, London NW1 3BH

Orchard Books Australia

Level 17/207 Kent Street, Sydney, NSW 2000

First published in 2011 by Orchard Books

Text © Margaret Mayo 2011

Illustrations © Alex Ayliffe 2011

The rights of Margaret Mayo to be identified as the author

and of Alex Ayliffe to be identified as the illustrator of this work

have been asserted by them in accordance with the

Copyright, Designs and Patents Act, 1988.

A CIP catalogue record for this book

is available from the British Library.

ISBN 978 1 40831 250 6

1 3 5 7 9 10 8 6 4 2

Printed in China

Orchard Books is a division of Hachette Children's Books,

an Hachette UK company.

www.hachette.co.uk